Vulture Verses

Love Poems for the Unloved

Written by Diane Lang
Illustrated by Lauren Gallegos

Dedicated to my four favorite turkey vultures—
Richard, Diablo, Prince, and Torac
— D.L.
To my husband, who helps me seek Beauty in all things
— L.G.

Text copyright © 2012 by Diane Lang
Illustrations © 2012 by Lauren Gallegos

Published by Prospect Park Media
969 S. Raymond Avenue
Pasadena, California 91105
www.prospectparkmedia.com

Library of Congress Cataloging in Publication Data
Lang, Diane.
Vulture verses : love poems for the unloved / written by Diane Lang ; illustrated by Lauren Gallegos. -- 1st ed.
p. cm.
Summary: Illustrated poems that help children understand the good things done by animals that are scary or unusual.
ISBN 978-0-9834594-5-3
1. Animals--Juvenile poetry. 2. Children's poetry, American. I. Gallegos, Lauren, ill. II. Title.
PS3612.A5494V85 2012
811'.6--dc23
2012002823

First edition, first printing

Designed by Lauren Gallegos. Manufactured in China.

Production Location: Everbest Printing Company, Guangdong, China
Production Date: March 8, 2012
Cohort: Batch 106589

I'm writing friendship notes! I love sending cards to all my friends, and I don't want to forget anyone. But look outside! I see someone who probably never gets a note or birthday card or even a valentine. I'm going to send a card to him and to all our other secret friends.

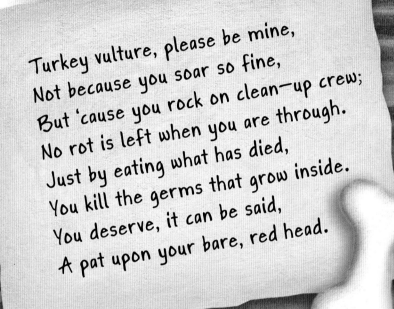

Turkey vulture, please be mine,
Not because you soar so fine,
But 'cause you rock on clean—up crew;
No rot is left when you are through.
Just by eating what has died,
You kill the germs that grow inside.
You deserve, it can be said,
A pat upon your bare, red head.

Turkey vultures not only clean up carrion (yes, dead stuff)
but their digestive systems kill any germs that may be there.
They keep animals—and maybe us—from getting sick.

Little mole, you leave a hole,
But you have a bigger role.
You sift the dirt as you proceed,
To hunt each bug or centipede.
You don't eat plants or tender shoots.
You leave alone the growing roots.
You look solely for the critters
That might serve as mole-y fritters:
Cutworm larvae, beetles too,
Who might eat our gardens through.
And you mix the healthy dirt
(And really, does one mole hill hurt?
Or even more; they can be flattened),
As our mole friends become fattened
On that dinner underground.
So please, dear mole, do stick around!

The rumors about moles eating plants is not true! They really eat the bugs (and slugs) that cause the plant damage. They might make your lawn look less than perfect where they push the dirt from their burrows to the surface, but they do no harm.

Spider, I could give you hugs
Because you eat those garden bugs
And insects who might sting or bite.
But I won't try to squeeze you tight,
Lest I squash a friend so fine.
So go on spinning out your line
Of silk to catch those insects who
Gobble leaves my garden through.

If it weren't for spiders, we would be up to our knees in insects. If you find a spider in your house, help it safely outside so it can keep up its good work.

Skunk, although you sometimes stink,
You're sweeter than most people think,
Because you eat each buggy pest
That thinks my garden tastes the best.
You chomp each beetle on the vine.
So be, dear skunk, my valentine.

Skunks eat large numbers of insects that are considered harmful to humans. They especially like cockroaches, and often dig up and eat yellowjacket larvae.

Oh fly, though no one thinks to ask,
Recycling is your secret task.
You eat the things that die or spoil
And make them part of growing soil.
So, though I shoo you from my plate,
You're someone I appreciate!

Flies are specialists at eating things that are dead and decaying,
getting them ready to become part of new, healthy soil.

Dear snake, some people run or yelp.
Instead, I thank you for your help.
You guard our food—from beans to rice—
By eating all those rats and mice.
So I'll not fuss; I'll let you be.
Please slither on, with love from me.

They may be unfamiliar, or even scary, to us, but snakes are very important in keeping nature's balance. And only 10 to 15% of snake species worldwide are venomous.

Jay, you can be naughty, bird!
But still I loved you when I heard
That some lost acorns that you hide
Will sprout new oak trees far and wide,
Which then give shade where each bough bends,
And homes for other feathered friends.

Jays sometimes rob other birds' nests, but they are responsible for the growth of new trees for more nests. They hide acorns and other nuts, and sometimes forget where they put them. Many forgotten ones sprout and grow into trees.

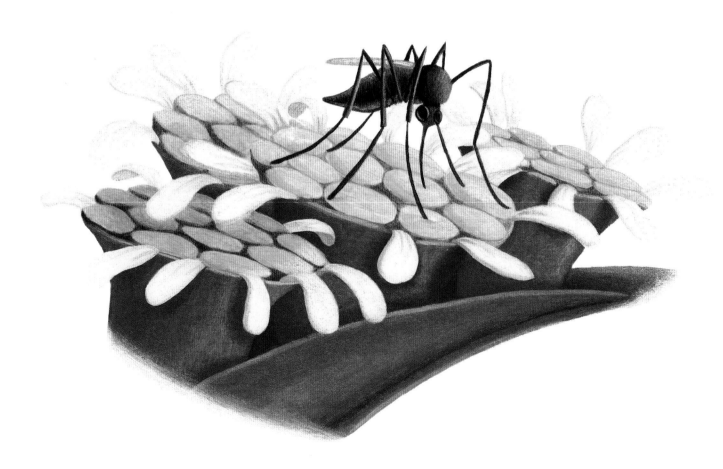

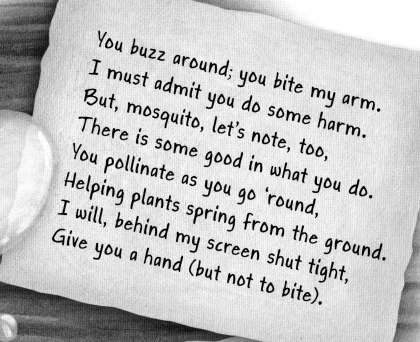

You buzz around; you bite my arm.
I must admit you do some harm.
But, mosquito, let's note, too,
There is some good in what you do.
You pollinate as you go 'round,
Helping plants spring from the ground.
I will, behind my screen shut tight,
Give you a hand (but not to bite).

Yes, even mosquitoes have their place. Like many other insects, they pollinate (and only the females bite).

"Reduce, reuse, recycle" is what we're s'posed to do,
Using things yet once again and making old things new.
And you're the champ of doing that, dear cockroach on the ground.
You munch what rots on forest floor, wherever dead stuff's found.
You make things into smaller bits for turning into soil.
A big, big job for little you; thanks for all your toil!
(But may I say, now that we're here, though you can glow with pride,
We recycle on our own; please don't come inside.)

Cockroaches have a very important role in maintaining the energy cycle that returns nutrients from dead plants and animals to the soil.

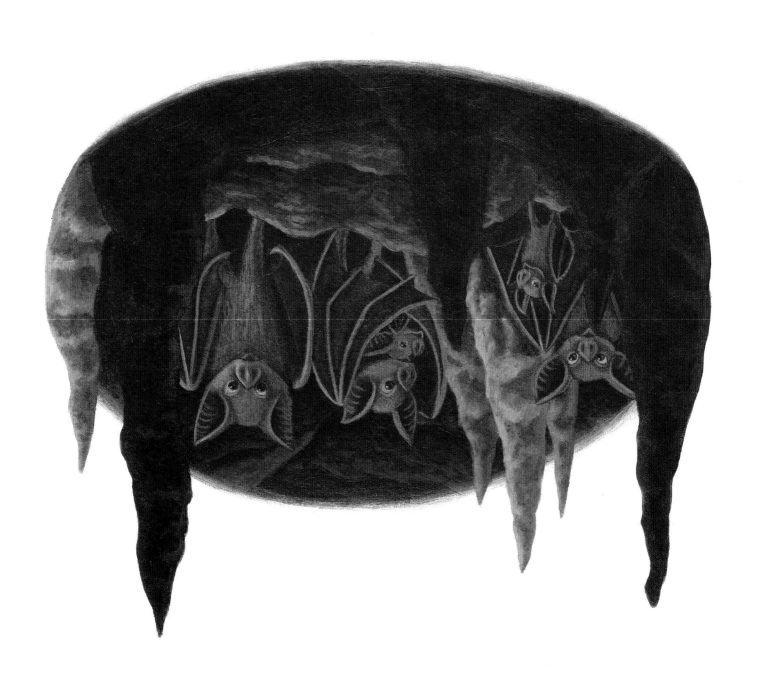

How kind you are, oh vampire bat.
We need to copy good deeds that
You do for others in your group,
Like giving hungry friends some "soup,"
And taking orphans to your care.
Though small, you're big enough to share.
You live a way that does inspire,
And so I praise you, and admire.

These tiny flying mammals of Central and South America share food with other bats in the colony who did not get enough to eat (yes, they regurgitate their blood meal) and adopt others' orphans. Their saliva makes their small bite painless to the cattle or chickens they take blood from; they are rarely interested in the blood of humans.

Your stinger is like Cupid's arrow:
Very sharp and very narrow,
But sharpness doesn't quite compare
With what you give us from the air.
I love the blooms you pollinate,
The honey sweet upon my plate.
So I'll ignore your sharpest end,
Because, dear bee, you're such a friend.

Do you like melons? Peaches? Pears? Bees pollinate these fruits,
and many more, gathering pollen as they seek out sweet nectar.
We owe them a big thank you.

I love you bat; you eat, in main,
Those moths who dine on fields of grain.
And then mosquitoes you devour,
Sometimes six hundred in an hour.
Some bats, straight to the fruit you go.
When you drop seeds, more fruit will grow.
So thanks for eating what you do—
My loving heart goes out to you.

Without bats, we would be harvesting much less grain, including the wheat, rice, and corn we need to make bread, cereal, and other food. Bats use echolocation to grab hungry moths (and mosquitoes!) right out of the air.

On nighttime visits 'possums go,
Searching down each garden row,
For snails and slugs they find sublime;
So, dear opossum, please be mine.
Come through my garden any day
Or night, I mean—your time to play.

These nocturnal marsupials are omnivores—they eat everything!
They are especially fond of plant-eating snails and slugs, so
gardeners can welcome a visit from them.

So many more cards to write! So many animal friends! I may
need some help. Do you know someone who is misunderstood?
Will you help me write some friendship notes, too?

"There is nothing ugly in nature. The seeming exceptions are simply facts of beauty we have not yet grasped."
—*Freeman Tilden*